Latchkey Tales
Vol 1.2 Elementals (Children of Water)

Edited by

Jax Goss

Solarwyrm Press

Published by Solarwyrm Press, 2014
www.solarwyrm.com
Copyright 2014 Solarwyrm Press
Each story © 2014 for their respective authors
Cover Design by Luke Spooner
All Rights Reserved
ISBN 978-0-9941106-2-6

Contents

Introduction

Water is powerful. It is fundamental to life, but can also bring gasping choking death. It can change landscapes over time, drip-dripping, wearing away at the earth, making valleys and carving itself through rock. It can be soft and cool and soothing, and it can be violent and passionate and all-consuming.

Myths abound with stories of the beings that live in water – merpeople, sirens, strange creatures and monsters and beautiful, dangerous beings. If you walk down to the water's edge, you stand in liminal space – the line between worlds. The sea laps at your feet with promises of otherworldliness, whispers of magic and life and death.

The stories and poems in this volume address all aspects of water – the beautiful and the dangerous, the terrifying and the empowering. Some will make you smile, some will make you soar, some will disturb you, leave you wondering what's hidden in those expanses of water about which we know so little.

Children of water. Some are human, some are not. Some are something in between. All will creep inside your head, curl up and make themselves at home, haunting you long after you've closed the book and set it aside.

Welcome, dear reader. Dive in. Find out what

is hiding beneath the surface. Come swim beneath the waves. Try not to drown.

Jax Goss
Dunedin, July 2014

And the Key Sang

Joel A. Nichols

*A man who is about to repeat
the risky stunt he successfully
completed years before realises
what it will cost him.*

Wooden steps fall down a stone wall, thirty narrow planks that drop into a landing, then thirty more, a landing, thirty more, a landing, thirty more, a landing. Grooves run up and down the chalky walls moist with beads of cool stone sweat. The City has strung electric lights in orange birdcages that cast long blue-green shadows up the wall toward daylight. At the bottom of the stairs there rests a wooden walkway on a shelf of slimy limestone. The shelf is just wide enough for the walkway, the walkway just wide enough for the crowd of men three and four deep, their backs pressed up against those clammy walls. Off the far end of the walkway, a man stands out on the timber post, looking down into the water. A swollen rope snakes off the post and slips under the edge of black water. A key dangles at the end of the thick rope too deep for the men to see, and flits like a minnow.

Somewhere in the crowd of men a bottle tips

up to somebody's lips and then to somebody else's. A man leans over the edge of the planks, looses a piss into the water. These men have been waiting for hours, in place before the man out on the post had trudged down the wooden steps, working his way slowly through the gut of the crowd. And now that he's out there, they wait for him to dive.

Thirty-four years ago since that same man—a wiry, tight boy then—had dived for the key, dived down those hundreds of feet along the slimy rope and snatched the dappled key. A sixteen year old Greek boy had done it, in 1904. After whom three had drowned themselves trying: a nineteen year old Scot, in 1973, a twenty four year old Finn in 1980, a sixteen year old Filipino in 1988. All of them had puffed up their chests and pulled themselves under, hand over hand along the rope. Two of them—1973, 1980—had blacked out under that undulating blanket and floated lazily dead to the surface within ten minutes. In 1988, the sixteen year old had shot back to the surface gasping. He hadn't gotten the key and the pressure had started an aneurysm. He flopped against the wooden walkway as the crowd flattened its back against the cool stone walls, bleeding out droplets of that same underground water.

In a hundred years, two have reached the bottom of the rope and made it back up with the key, the sixteen year old in 1904, and the man standing out on the post now. Every few minutes a camera flash washes away the long blue-green shadows for a blinding second and leaves the men packed in along the walkway seeing a snatch of rainbow fish floating at eyeball's edge.

Our diver, on his first attempt: glowing brown skin, leg hair bleached gold on chicken-breast thighs sticking out of cut off denims with tangles of cotton thread, straggly hair knotted up in a lumpy bun. Short torso and a concave slope from the top of his shorts up to his rib cage. When he raised his arms to dive, thirty-odd years ago, his tanned skin pulled sheath-taut over each costal, ligaments bending toward the splash. The crowd didn't breath at first, but as the seconds slipped into a minute, they took a breath, an exchange of air the man underneath couldn't take. And two minutes tocked, and then the third. A mosquito buzz rose in the crowd, a shshshing that he was dead. The clock went to four just as his arm plunged through, breaking the tension in concentric circles. Treading water with one hand and both feet, gasping and waving above his head the pulpy end of rope and the gold-coloured key blooming red and blue oxidation stains.

The crowd shifted in his direction. One or two of the men tiptoeing the edge of the walkway tripped into the frigid water and were hauled back up with the diver.

Perhaps some of the men who crowd there now were there in 1972. In this City, the men look alike and talk alike and smell alike so even if they are not the *same* they are the same.

Our diver, now: poised on the timber. Short brown shorts rolled up so they are even shorter, turtlenecking the top of his legs that still look meaty and powerful; his skin is scored with lines fine and thick, vertical and horizontal, and has the shiny brown yellow of old burns. His hair is still knotty, is still dirty, is still screwed to the back of his head in a messy Samurai button, but it's gray. Green tracings of a blurry tattoo paisley his back and his shoulder. Somewhere in the design sits a square-toothed key. His ear is pierced, the hole stretched around the sharp point of a brown Amazon-basin arrowhead, and he has a skin knife tied just below his left kneecap.

After the thirty-four year old Greek in 1974, our diver gave a radio interview that blamed the City for those deaths. *It's reckless*, he said; *makes boys who can swim think they can claim that key. The City should haul up that rope and throw away that key.*

But the key had been down there forever. Whenever a boy was able to haul up—they started keeping hit or miss records in the 1880s—he'd get to wear the key for a day and then he would have to tie it to the end of the rope and toss it back into the pool.

The radio interviewer had asked about the key. If it had given him pleasure, holding a key that was so important to the whole City but which had been worn by only tens of men. The tape crackles when he says it was not worth it.

But he'd also won money, from a tavernist at whose bar he drank the night he wore the key.

And now this time, a foreign beer corporation had promised more money. Enough for a retirement, which, for the diver, means a tiny house without a mortgage. Out on the timber, he takes another slow breath. He's watching the smooth surface, peering

7

into the black. He's trying to spot the key. He thinks:

I'm going to die.

It'll be a blackout, probably after I've grabbed the key.

The night he had worn the key, he had whatever he wanted. Every woman and child in the village wanted to touch it, and had come up, giggling, to stretch out a finger and tickle the cold metal against his chest. Older boys and men, too, but they don't sidle up shying behind a flattened palm. They marched up, and clapped him on the back with one hand and cup the key dangling around his neck. And bowls and bowls of tart wine and bitter anise spirits and as much food as he could eat. The money, too, from the tavernist.

But then the tavern had closed and he was alone with it. The key longed for the darkness of the pool. It longed for the tension pull as the twine slipped down from the timber post. It longed for water, and for quiet. And what the key sang, the diver wants. What the key sang, the diver became, for the whole night through until the men of the town lined up to watch him tether key to twine, to timber, and let it drop. But he was the only one who heard it singing on the way down, singing for him to follow.

The money is what's brought him back. Without it, he will drift from woman to woman who lets him stay in one corner of her bed and eat from her pots until he blows away. The day labouring, vegetable and fruit harvests, house painting, part of a roofing crew on one of the big buildings coming up in the new part of the City: all of it leaving him a pocketful of coins and bills to leave for the woman keeping him less only a mason jar of spirits every week or so. If he can snatch the key again...

But he still hears the singing. The diver holds up his hand and turns around. He steps off the timber post and into the crowd, which is rustling a murmur, whispers of disbelief. And he pushes his way through the gaping men, pushing toward daylight.

About Joel A. Nichols

Joel A. Nichols has recent stories in *With: New Gay Fiction* and the first issue of the weird fiction magazine *Phobos*, as well as reviews and fiction on *Chelsea Station*, an online magazine. He is a library branch manager, and has also written two professional books for librarians (*iPads in the Library* (2013) and *Teaching Internet Basics* (2014)), both from Libraries Unlimited, and is currently a member of the Stonewall Book Award jury. Joel studied German at Wesleyan University, Creative Writing at Temple University with Samuel R. Delany, and Library Science at Drexel. He lives in Philadelphia with his boyfriend and their child.

Water in Her Eyes

Shauna Aura Knight

Water in her eyes
Sorrowful weeping pouring of tears
Fathomless seas, rivers, lakes
The Chalice is in her eyes
Her eyes are the seas where I am born and I die
The water holds me
She pours out her light in liquid tears
Pouring over me, bathing me, blessing me
Holding me, purifying me
What is this water I see the water of a thousand seas
weeping
Heaven in her eyes
Lost in her eyes
Comfort in her eyes
Angel eyes
Eyes of peace and love
Eyes like a womb to nourish and comfort
The water an embryonic fluid to hold me—
"You were never alone," she says
And I feel it wrapped in the warmth of
Her dark sea

ABOUT SHAUNA AURA KNIGHT

Shauna Aura Knight is an author, artist, presenter and mystic seeker. Her poetry, art, and other work is inspired by awakening mythic imagination and the stories of heroes and of the darkness we each must overcome. She's the author of several urban fantasy and paranormal romance novels. She's also published numerous articles and several books on personal transformation, spiritual seeking, leadership, and facilitation, and travels nationally, speaking on those topics. www.shaunaauraknight.com

The Collector

Tara Campbell

*Being Trident's girlfriend
isn't as glamorous as one would
think—a mermaid tries to make the
most of her banishment far away
from the ocean.*

The mermaid wriggled up toward the surface of her lake, eyes fixed on a silver object floating above her. She hovered below the shiny cylinder and plucked it down from its perch between water and air. It was a beer can, dented but still closed. She put it in her plastic shopping bag and dove all the way down to the murky bottom of the lake.

She glided over the bed of silt below, careful not to cloud her vision by stirring up sludge. The dull glint of something metal inside a flowing tangle of grasses caught her eye. She pulled at the weeds and extracted a knife. It was a pocketknife this time, smaller than the switchblade she'd found before, perhaps easier to handle. Triton had been so upset when she'd cut herself slicing water grasses—but not upset enough to move her out of this lake he'd put her in. He was like that, concerned enough to keep her away from all the Mrs. Tritons, but not enough to marry her. He said he'd already hit his wife limit at

5,000. She'd never known of a god with a wife limit, or any other limit for that matter. She folded the pocketknife and slipped it into her bag.

A slight change in current caught her attention. She listened to the water, picking up tiny vibrations that seemed to be coming from the far shore. Lake weed floated and bowed while young carp chased each other around her waist. The vibrations stopped, then started again. The mermaid waved the fish away and went to investigate, the pocketknife and can of beer bumping against her flank as she swam. It took her several minutes, swimming fast, to reach the other end. Triton had wanted her to be comfortable, choosing a lake deep and wide enough for her to swim, play and receive his visits without being discovered.

· The water shuddered again. She stopped behind a thick clutch of reeds and put a hand to the bottom of the lake. The heft and timing of the thumping felt like it was coming from grown humans, heavy ones. Probably men. After several minutes the thumping stopped. Quiet. Then came the worm, impaled on a hook.

Breakfast.

The mermaid waited for the hook to sink. She took it gingerly by the eye, slid the worm off and popped it in her mouth. Then she gave the line a good strong tug, yanking her hand away as the metal barb shot upward.

She scanned the water for a second hook. There was always a second one. A moment later she found it, swished up to it and downed the second worm. By then, the first hook had reappeared with fresh bait, which she also snatched and shared with one of the carp that had begun to join her. She batted the fish away from the hooks, as much to get first dibs on the worms as to keep the fish from getting snagged. The carp were the closest thing she had to company.

The fishermen fed a few more worms into the lake before giving up. She stayed absolutely still—still enough to hear muffled talking and laughter filter through the water. With a rush of adrenaline, she let herself flirt with the surface, allowing the tip of her tail to flash above water for seconds at a time. Triton had warned her not to let anyone see her. With all the thought he had put into the shape of her lake and its places to hide, she wondered how he could have forgotten the most important variable: curiosity. That "What-Would-Happen-If?" impulse that neither humankind nor mermankind could resist. This was, it occurred to her, a rather large factor not to have considered; especially since it was something she and Triton shared—and was what had eventually landed her in this lake.

The tingle of imminent danger faded when she heard the men thump to their vehicle and drive away. As the vibrations waned, she swam over to her secluded spot on the other side of the lake, beer can in tow. She kept going past the point where the tips of the weeping willow brushed the top of the water. Once behind the curtain of greenery, she broke the surface of the water and wriggled up onto her favourite rock.

She pulled the can of beer out and opened it, taking a first, long drink. Carp circled her rock and she alternated sipping from the can and pouring beer shots into the lake for the fish. She couldn't tell what they were thinking, really, but she hoped they could share in her sunny, happy stupor.

The mermaid decided she was in the mood for a cigarette. Downing the rest of the beer, she slipped back into the lake, heading for her stash on land. She pulled herself partway out of the water near a small cave-cache, shaking the drops from her hands before pulling the grass overhang aside. She grabbed one of the cigarettes she'd skimmed off the surface of the lake and left there to dry. Sticking the crumpled butt into her mouth, she flipped open a small, mangled matchbook she'd found on the shore. It was empty! She ripped the cigarette out of her mouth and threw it back into the cache, flopping onto her back and crossing her arms.

As intent as she was on brooding, her concentration was broken by a *click*. Then another one.

She looked out from the shadows behind the weeping willow and saw the back of a boy crouching by the shore. Children often caught her by surprise. Unless they were running, she never felt them coming.

The mermaid wanted to know what the boy was doing, but would have to get closer to see. She slipped into the lake and glided closer, then surfaced only up to the eyes. The boy was still too engrossed in what he was doing to notice her. She inched out from behind the curtain of willow branches, eyes above the water, angling to observe him from the side.

Her heartbeat quickened when she finally saw what he was looking at. It was one of those little rockets, the kind children put in a bottle and light and run. She never got tired of these tiny fireworks, with their sense of danger in miniature. Eyes glued to the rocket, she held her breath, anticipating the crackle of the fuse, the *whoosh* of flight, the *pop!* in the air.

She wouldn't mind having the lighter either. But it didn't seem to work—or was he just not using it correctly? She heard *click* and *click* and *click*, but the fuse wouldn't light. Then the clicking stopped. She looked up and met the boy's eyes.

She twisted downward in a frenzied dive, knowing it was too late. The boy's face peered over the edge of the lake, looming above her through the stream of bubbles she had created. She kept telling Triton this lake was too small; that too many children came here to play. That this was all his fault.

She looked up again and saw the shadow of the boy's head above her. She imagined him on his hands and knees, leaning out over the water, craning his neck to catch another glimpse of her, teetering uncertainly over the edge.

*

That evening the mermaid sat on her favourite rock, smoking a stubby cigarette. She watched the carp slide past one another in the water, knowing she had only one or two more days of peace before the men would come to look for the boy.

One of the carp jumped out of the water onto her rock. It lay still, its mouth opening and closing, gaping again and again as it watched her.

"I know, I'm sorry," she said, and nudged the fish back into the water with the tip of her tail. Soon the men would come to search the shore, then dredge the lake—and now she had one more carp to keep out of harm's way when they arrived.

About Tara Campbell

Tara Campbell [www.taracampbell.com] is a Washington, D.C.-based writer of crossover sci-fi. With a BA in English and an MA in German Language and Literature, she has a demonstrated aversion to money and power. Her stories have appeared in *Lorelei Signal*, *Punchnel's*, *GlassFire Magazine*, the *WiFiles*, *Silverthought Online*, *Toasted Cake Podcast*, *Litro Magazine*, *Luna Station Quarterly*, *Up, Do: Flash Fiction by Women Writers*, *T. Gene Davis's Speculative Blog*, *Master's Review* and *SciFi Romance Quarterly*.

Adie

Jax Goss

Five year olds know things.
Adie knows that it's true.
He's been watching that puddle
For an hour or two.

Five year olds know things.
She read it somewhere.
She peeked over his shoulder
And there's nothing in there.

He's been watching that puddle
For three hours now,
And Adie can't shake the feeling
That it's dangerous somehow.

Adie's watching her brother,
Staring into the water.
Adie hopes that she right
'bout what all the books taught 'er.

Adie knows about monsters
She's a fan of Ms. Aching*.
Adie's learnt about fairies
And smelly cheese-making.

When the thing in the puddle
Reaches out to the air,
When the thing in the puddle
Tries to pull him down there,

Adie knows that she'll have
But a moment to act,
To rescue her brother,
Only seconds in fact.

But Adie is ready.
When it tries to take Dan,
She'll smack that damned thing
With a cast iron pan.

* Adie reads a lot of Terry Pratchett

About Jax Goss

Jax Goss is an editor and writer. She is a wandering South African who seems to have settled in New Zealand. She lives in Dunedin, for the moment. She is currently employed full time as the mother of a very small human, and writes and edits on the side. She expects this situation to stay the same for a while, but she has long ago learnt that nothing ever goes the way she expects.

She spends a large amount of her time gathering tales and poems and art and sending them out into the world in various forms, and thinks that this may be her vocation. You can follow her wayward journey at her website: jaxgoss.wordpress.com.

Sugarplum Island

Barb Siples

Too old for his orphanage, a mysterious foundling is kicked to the streets of a derelict manufactory town and lured into paradise.

The door was broad, heavy oak and David Smith stood on the wrong side of it. The summer sun glinted along a plaque fixed to the crossbeam. It read: *St. Bartholomew's Home for Orphans*.

"I could help out," David said to the tall man with the priest's collar who barred the threshold. "With the chores. Laundry. Cooking."

Behind David the listless traffic of the street clattered past, ramshackle carts trailed by stiff-legged dogs and louse-bitten children, equally feral. The noontime odour of boiled cabbage overwhelmed the usual taint of sewage in the air.

Father Joseph stood firm before the closed door. "Those tasks are for the sisters to do."

"Gardening, then. Or fixing things. I could turn wood in the shop."

"You can't step foot in the shop without having a fit. All the dust and it's worse around plants. Your lungs are weak, David. It's a cross you've been given to bear."

"But I'll do anything. Please let me stay."

Father Joseph knotted his steely eyebrows. "Do you love this place so much?"

No, David did not. He flinched through the halls and dormitories of St. Bartholomew's like an unwelcome guest. The other inmates taunted him for his odd looks, eyes set too far apart on his face, hair lank and dark as weeds, skin that never browned beneath the sun. Even the sisters looked at him askance, whispering about the frantic dreams that woke the other children.

"Well?" demanded Father Joseph.

David couldn't decide how best to answer. He bore no love for St. Bartholomew's but had little hope things would be different elsewhere. In his heart lay a craving for home equal to the force that guides the journey of sea turtles to the sands of their birth, the great migration of whales. But David's yearning was a desire without a destination, an ache that would never mend.

"I want..." he began but had no words to describe the magnitude of what he lacked.

"You knew this day would come," Father Joseph said as he backed toward the door. "You're nearly a man grown, twelve years old I should think. Try the docks. There's bound to be work at the waterfront." The priest turned away.

David lunged for the doorknob and a brief struggle ensued. Father Joseph prevailed and slipped inside. The *snick* of the deadbolt sounded a moment

24

later.

David rattled the doorknob and shouted and slapped his palm against the unyielding wood. No one paid any attention. The sun pinched his temples and made eels of water slide down his neck and past his collar. The heat robbed him of breath.

David gave up on the door and wiped the sting of salt from his eyes with a much-mended sleeve. It was hard to think what to do. As cheerless as it was, David had no notion of himself outside of the orphanage. Even the name he bore had been assigned to him by St. Bartholomew's administrators.

One thing was certain, no matter what Father Joseph advised. David would not go near the docks. The port was a nightmare of fear and confusion, a tangle of oars and fishing lines, of gulls screaming overhead and beach sand scouring his skin. He wouldn't go uptown either. The wealthy hired doormen to keep people like David from disturbing them. He knew that from the scabby men who came now and then to beg scraps from the sisters.

That left mid-town, the sprawling grid of cottages and enterprises that buffered the mansions of the rich from the faltering industry of the waterfront. With a last look at the sunlight glinting from the nameplate of his erstwhile refuge, David stepped into the street. The endless parade of desperation parted ranks, wary but unperturbed by his solitary calamity.

He came to a bakery whose paint peeled less noticeably than the shops around it and poked his head inside. No, he wasn't filching. He wanted work.

Yes, he was in earnest. There was no reason to laugh like that, the baker could have simply said no. The tailor gave him worse, a push out the door and a swish of his leather measuring tape. David knew better than to raise a protest. Things always got worse when he drew a crowd.

The road sloped down and David walked until blisters stung his instep. Everywhere it was the same. No one was hiring. He began to see terrible possibilities in the landscape of doorways and culverts and sewer drains he passed, places he would never before have considered shelter.

"Hello, my love," a shrill voice said. "Come say hello to Sally, my striking young man."

A lady with painted lips and painted cheeks and a very low bodice stepped from the mouth of an alley. She motioned him over with her finger. David joined her and saw that several women stood in the shadows, lounging against doorways in the dingy half-light.

"He *is* a remarkable looking lad," said one, dark where Sally was fair, but painted and dressed the same. "Come 'ere, love. Have you coins to spend on sweet Mabel?"

"I'm from St. Bart's," he said, confused by their lack of hostility. "I'm looking for work."

"I can think of work for a remarkable young man like you," Sally shrilled. Her skin sagged beneath the powder, like rotten fruit behind a dusting of sugar. "Those spooky, sea-green eyes. Some johns like a touch of the exotic. Eh, ladies?"

"Is there work?" David said and stepped

deeper into the alley. The skirts of the ladies flashed with colour as they sauntered toward him. They stroked his pale cheeks and ran their fingers through his dark, reedy hair. David stood still, afraid to believe they meant him no harm. Their hands slid beneath his shirt, up his chest, over his ribs.

"Ew!" said one and the hands stopped. "What's he got?"

David's shirt was tugged from his waistband and lifted up over his head. The women got a good look at the marks that scored his sides.

"What's that, lad? Scars?" Fingers traced the ridges over his ribcage.

"Yes. No. I don't know." David pulled away and tucked his shirt back in his trousers, poised to flee. But the women appeared to anticipate his answer. He said, "Father Joseph found me this way when I was a baby, after the storm of Twenty-Three. I was under a rowboat, washed halfway up the beach."

They stared at him. One of the ladies said, "I remember the 'Tempest of Twenty-Three.' Just a lass, I was. My dad had me selling nosegays to the tourists, back when we had tourists. Wind howled all night, nearly blew the roof off the cottage. In the morning folks came to help clean up. Found a porpoise halfway up Church Street. Dead, of course. Lots of fishermen too. You say you came up off the beach?"

David shook his head and clamped his arms over his ribs. "I'm from St. Bart's. The orphanage?"

Sally's eyes roamed his body. "We could use a boy. For our more... particular customers. Eh, ladies?"

"Let Ned have a look at 'im," Mabel said, and

called down the alleyway.

A pair of hulking shoulders separated from the shadows and came toward them. Ned had a nose like a smashed potato and the staring eyes of a goat. David couldn't look away from them. Ned's thick fingers seized hold of his collar. "You want to work for me? You want to be one of Ned's girls?"

David lunged like a marlin. A button popped and spun into the dark and David wrenched free.

"Fly, boy," Mabel hooted after him. "Or Ned'll have you."

When he could run no more, David sank down on the lip of a crumbling public fountain. A flame smouldered in his chest and flared whenever he took a breath. He pulled a rag out of his pocket and soaked it, then breathed through the wet fabric. Stupid to run like that. Running always set off an attack. He should not have stopped for the women. He knew better than to trust the appearance of kindness.

On the far side of the shabby square stood a statue of a man on a horse. A dent decorated the hero's bronze head and signs of an old fire scorched the stone plinth. Some boys David's age congregated around the memorial. David stood up and drifted warily toward the gathering. He might find safety in numbers, out in the open, as long as no one singled him out.

"Come one, come all," said a bony, wild-haired fellow, waving the crowd closer. "Diamond Jim wants you. You'll have work come morning."

"What kind of work?" called a boy from the crowd.

"Running coal. We need boys to run coal. Strong boys, like you."

"Pay's good, too," said a man leaning against the horse's metal flank. Scars puckered the skin of his crossed arms. More men loitered in the shade behind the statue. David didn't like the look of them, restless and predatory.

"There's a bun for luncheon," Diamond Jim said. "Just so, no charge. And a place to settle for the night. It's growing dark, lads. Come along with us."

David thought he might speak up but the moment passed. No one moved.

Jim whistled through his teeth. The men drifting in the shadows darted forward and circled the gathering. The crowd erupted in panic, boys thrashing and shoving. David felt a hand snag his hair and lost his footing. A knife-thin man whipped a cord around his wrists, fast as a fisherman with his reel, and hauled him to his feet. David bucked and dragged at the rope in terror. The constriction of his limbs and the inexorable tug felt horribly familiar, a nightmare sensation that squeezed his chest and turned his saliva to acid.

Diamond Jim's men drove him and three other captives through a maze of walkways that ran between a cluster of manufactories. A shed with crooked wooden slats for walls leaned against one of the brick buildings. The shed had a door and Jim turned the key in the lock once David and the others crouched inside. The boys wriggled free of their bonds. They stood staring at each other in the green illumination from the gas lamps that filtered through the gaps in the walls. David tried a smile.

"Stay away," one of the boys told him. "Don't come near us."

David retreated to a far corner. Whatever marked him could not be hidden, some unfavourable quality that lingered about his person like musk. He reached down in his trouser pocket, past the damp rag, for a little parcel wrapped in a scrap of cloth and tied with string. He loosed the knot and freed his treasure, a white seashell, to the eerie dusk.

David rubbed his thumbs over the ridged surface, flipped the shell over to watch the lamplight shimmer across the nacre. The elusive flicker of colour signified something long buried, irretrievable, a murmur just beyond comprehension... a soothing vastness without a name. He pressed his eye to the hole bored into the oval and peered out the other side. When Father Joseph had found him, a strand of seaweed threaded that little hole and secured the pendant to David's ankle. Now, in his prison of wood slats and packed earth, David drifted off to sleep, polishing the mystery of his past against his fingertips.

In the morning he was made to run coal.

Diamond Jim's associates conducted him and the other boys through a narrow manufactory door and into the basement, where the boiler stood. The brick walls rose high and grim, unrelieved by natural light. Oil lamps spread dusty shadows here and there. No windows meant little chance of an escape. David knew he wouldn't last long in such a place. But if he did as he was told he might become trusted—or at least ignored—and a way out would perhaps present itself.

The boys' job was to help the tender keep the furnace stoked. All that mattered was that the fire never slacked. Diamond Jim patrolled with a switch and made sure no one faltered. Waves of heat wriggled from the crucible and the workers stripped down to their underclothes. David was the only one who kept his ribs covered. Coal was delivered twice during the day and crashed down the chute with the roar of a landslide. David had a rake and he used it to push the black rocks toward the tenders and their shovels. Sometimes he and the other boys scrambled up and down the coal mountain with pails.

The dusty air seared David's throat, but Diamond Jim would hear neither excuses nor pleas. David took out his rag and wet it with water provided for the crew. After the break—David got a bun—he tied the rag around his nose and mouth. That worked some. But the fire in his chest outpaced the one in the furnace. His lungs battered his ribcage. David couldn't speak and he couldn't breathe. He stumbled on some loose coals and slid down the mountain. Diamond Jim dragged him outside and deposited him in a patch of rubble along the manufactory wall.

At quitting time David lay where Jim had left him. His lungs were working again, just sore, but he didn't get up. An appalling weariness fixed his limbs and smothered his will. Diamond Jim sat down beside him and ate the second bun of the day. David asked for some but Jim ignored him.

"I won't go back in the shed," David wheezed.

Diamond Jim rose without a word and went on his way. David lay on his back, his hand in his pocket. His skin itched beneath a layer of grime. He should get up and find a fountain, one that worked, and wash away the soot and sweat. He should find something to eat. David's hand moved in his pocket. The ridges of the shell consoled his fingertips and calmed his thoughts.

He woke from a dream in which tentacles snaked around his legs and bore him into deep water. Jim's fingers scrabbled at his ankle. David writhed on the litter-strewn ground and kicked at him, but his shoe came off in Jim's hand. David's other foot was bare already. Over his head, beyond the smokestacks, dawn spread like a bruise.

"Give me back my shoes!" David said.

Jim let out a whoop. "What's with your feet? Hey, fellas. Take a look."

David scrambled upright and away from the men who crowded round. The knife-thin fellow from the day before stared him in the eyes. "Freak," he said.

"Be off," Diamond Jim told him. "Be off with you."

David took his advice.

There was no reason to stay near the manufactory in any case. There was nowhere left for David to go except back to St. Bartholomew's. He would convince Father Joseph that he had done his best, but there was no place for him in the world. He would sit outside the door until he starved, or until the priest let him back in.

David started uphill, but the street wound and twisted on itself. This part of town was all labyrinthine alleys and giant buildings and chimney smoke. His eyes stung and watered and he coughed into his rag, blind to the path before him. A current of damp, savoury air penetrated the stifling heat and David blundered after it.

He turned a corner and stopped short at sight of the harbour. The tinkling of a hundred cheerful bells rose from the ships in their mooring. A breeze spun the coal dust from his hair, and the ocean blazed and sparkled beyond the seawall. David stared at the wriggling chimera of turquoise water. Why had he ever thought to fear the sea? The flavour of brine teased his tongue and brought a shivery recognition, a sensation of something precious being returned to him. David took a few heedless steps into the street.

"Steady on," a costermonger shouted and David stumbled out of his way. The man's cart overflowed with apples, fat and gold and luscious. David followed the wagon down to the waterfront, a confusion of sounds and colours and penetrating smells. Everywhere he looked vendors minded their stalls, hawking buns and biscuits and sausages. The perfume of grilled fish made his stomach gnaw his insides. David sidled over to a bustling counter. He would not starve to death, not now, not while the heave and slosh of the tide infused his blood with restlessness. Not when an array of sweetmeats rested mere inches from where he stood.

Now, while the owner was occupied. His hand reached out and whipped a morsel into his mouth.

Someone else's hand seized his wrist. David's gaze traveled up a row of shiny buttons in a faded blue coat.

"Whose boy are you?" the policeman said. His eyes were the same tired colour as the coat.

"Not anyone's, sir. Please. I need to get down there, down to the water. Let me go."

The copper had no intention of doing so and threatened violence if David failed to shut his hole. David shut it and did what he was told. This involved crouching in a locked wagon which rusted in an alley beside a cannery. All morning long David trembled to hear the rush and rumble of the waves. He longed for another glimpse of the sea, but the view from the single barred window showed him the damp brick of the opposite wall, oozing with mould. When the sun stood directly overhead and turned the inside of the wagon to an oven, the policeman returned. He brought company. Long yellow teeth and a sharp chin greeted David when he peered through the bars of his cage.

"Ain't none o' mine," the ratty man told the copper, turning from David's uneasy gaze. "Nor Harry Beaumont's neither. Brought me out for nothing, haven't you?"

"You lot can always use another one," the copper said. "Another set of nimble fingers. I'll have the usual fee for him. Same as would ransom one of your own."

"Nah," the man said.

"Why not?"

The other man shrugged.

34

"Beaumont'll snatch him up if you don't."

The yellow teeth grew longer as the thief-keeper smiled. "Cause of them nimble fingers? Caught him red-handed, did you not say?"

The copper swore and stalked off down the alleyway. David retreated from the window and sank back into the gloom of the wagon. He could well imagine the place the ratty man ruled over. It would be like St. Bartholomew's, without the intervention of the sisters. Even the waning of the men's footfalls as they departed could not calm his apprehension. Perhaps the officer would return with Mr. Beaumont. David would be forced to follow him to his den.

But as the long hours of the day progressed, David's chest began to rise and fall in rhythm with the surf. The pulse of the ocean ebbed and swelled and overwhelmed his blood. The tide changed and the relentless tug of the moon drew away his fear and loneliness. Shadows swallowed the inside of wagon when the clatter of the key in the lock roused him.

"Let me go," David told the officer. "I'm no thief, sir. I don't belong here."

"You won't be lingering. Going to Sugarplum Island, aren't you?"

"Island? You mean—? The water?" David surged from the wagon and the copper had to snatch his collar to slow him down.

David walked with the policeman across the gritty street and climbed onto the pier. The wood smelled damp and soft with evening. The dark and the waves and the briny air called to him in some voiceless way he couldn't define. He stepped light and tranquil into the triangular prow of the little boat tied to the piling below him. David understood now it was not the sea that must be feared, but the realm of rocks and shore, the peril of the fisherman's net.

The copper unshipped the oars and cast off from the stern. Two men sat slumped in the boat between the policeman and David.

"Sir?" David said. "This man here is bleeding. I think he's unconscious."

The policeman kept rowing. After a moment he said, "There's a good doctor on Sugarplum Island."

"Boy," whispered the man sitting next to him. He stank of liquor. "Untie me, boy." He held up his wrists, neatly bound with sisal. His ankles were tied together too.

"My dad was a sailor," the policeman said from the stern. The whites of his eyes flashed in the dark. "That knot won't budge."

The bound man cursed and squirmed.

"That won't help either. Nothing helps these days. Gaol's not big enough to hold all of you. Got to get rid of you somehow."

"It's murder," growled the drunkard. "Might be I'm a man past hope but I never murdered no one."

"Shut it," said the copper. "Or I'll stuff a rag in."

"What's he mean, sir?" David asked the officer. "Are we not all to find a new home on...?" His lips formed the unlikely name of their destination but no sound came from David's throat. There was no refuge waiting for him. Fire ignited in his chest and his breath came in gasps. David retreated as he was able, pressing his body into the narrow space of the prow.

His fingers pulled his treasure from his pocket and he held the white shell in front of his eyes, turning it over and over in his fingers. The boat lurched and slid across the choppy water.

The copper shipped the oars and let the boat rock on the waves. He took a metal flask from his boot and drank from it. He took the truncheon from his belt. He ignored the unconscious man with the bloody head. The drunkard closed his eyes as the copper shifted toward him. The sound of the wood against the prisoner's skull was like a crack of lightning. One after the other, the two limp men slipped from the copper's arms into the ocean.

David stood up in the prow, struggling for breath.

"It won't hurt," the copper told him. "It's that quick."

David held up his treasure, held it up and out in both hands. He could see the copper's face through the hole in the pendant. The moon shone on the white curve of the shell and made it glow. David could see the path of light on the water, a shimmering road that led straight to the boat, straight to him. He could see shapes moving beneath the waves, traveling, hurrying, rising, and there was not much time left. The copper raised his truncheon.

Wood splintered as something struck the side of the boat. Water exploded along the prow. David's arms flew over his head and he tumbled overboard. A vast, gelatinous form boiled from the depths and caught him up. Tentacles wrapped around his legs and hugged his waist and pulled him down. He wasn't frightened in the least.

David expanded his chest and breathed. The seams along his ribs parted like lips and sifted the air from the brine. The fire in his lungs went out. Water seethed under his skin and soothed his core. The tentacles slid away. The being known as David jackknifed after the dark presence, his legs kicking in sure, powerful strokes. His webbed toes found purchase on the sea-path of the current. All about him lithe bodies stirred the murky water, creatures born like David to the sea. A star-field glittered in the sandy floor below him, a hundred thousand white shells and more, guiding him, leading him, calling him home.

ABOUT BARB SIPLES

When not designing survival strategies for the
imminent planet-wide zombie apocalypse, Barb
Siples writes fiction from her fortified bunker in
The People's Republic of Portland, Oregon. You
can read more of her stuff at barbsiples.com.

The Siren Calls

Dominica Malcolm

Standing, frozen.
Filling his ears,
a haunting song.
The voice calls to
his deepest fears:

She loves you not,
so come with me;
I will show you
the path to home...
beneath the sea.

Step by step he's
drawn through the sand,
charmed... enchanted.
Moments later,
he leaves the land.

Blue scales, fins,
bare flesh, pink breast.
Awareness dawns,
too late. Water
fills his dark chest.

It's her, the blonde.
She'd been ashore;
her tail gone,
traded for legs.
Completely raw.

In this moment,
the cursed man knows,
the siren sings,
captures her prey,
where the tide goes.

ABOUT DOMINICA MALCOLM

Dominica Malcolm is a writer, stand-up comedian, filmmaker, and world traveller. She has previously worked with Solarwyrm to publish her pirate time-travel novel, *Adrift*, as well as the anthology, *Amok*, featuring Asia-Pacific speculative fiction. Though born in Australia, she spent five and a half years in Malaysia, and currently resides in the San Francisco Bay Area in California. To find out more about Dominica, visit her web site at http://dominica.malcolm.id.au

Wisdom

Llanwyre Laish

*A woman who pursues a fish
for fourteen years learns that she
can only catch what she desires
when she embodies it completely.*

It took her fourteen years to catch the fish. Day in, day out, she sat on the rock near the shore with her pole or her net and waited. While other girls from her village married and had children, she sat on the rock in the wind and the rain and waited for the fish. The weather ruined her face, her arms, her hands. Although the villagers had admired her beauty when she was young, they soon came to think of her obsession as ugly, and over time, her countenance came to match.

The seasoned fishermen laughed at her and advised her in equal amounts. She'd never catch from the rock, she'd never catch with that pole, and she'd never catch with a net. They'd never seen a fish there, in fact, in the deep pool of water that collected under the mossy rock.

She saw—or believed she saw—what they did not: the darting, silver glint of the fish deep underwater.

When she went inside her family's tiny cottage at night, she dreamt of fish.

Eventually, even she realised the folly of her approach. She climbed down from the rock and stood in the pool with her net, the freezing water covering her skinny legs as she pulled her skirts up around her waist. She could feel something moving, flicking around her feet, caressing her legs as she stood in the pool. She closed her eyes and tried to memorise its movements, but it remained too erratic, too ephemeral.

She knew the story: consuming the fish gave you wisdom, but if you let someone cook it for you, they were likely to eat it first, not intentionally, but somehow accidentally, a piece of fat or a drop of sauce burning a fingertip or falling onto a cuff and getting licked or sucked until the fish held no more of its power.

She didn't intend to let anyone cook the fish for her.

Time passed. Her family fed and clothed her, making sure she had what she needed, thinking of her obsession as the sad shadow of an unhealthy mind. She rose at daybreak and went to bed after dark, eating only a bit of bread and cheese at breakfast and lunch and growing thinner year by year. The children played around her during breaks in their school day, but they never dared throw anything or taunt her; they found her amusing, but they also feared her.

One little girl, the smallest and slowest in her class, stared at her longer than the others. While the other children laughed and played and danced near the pool, the girl simply stood there with her arms wrapped around her tiny body, rocking a little and watching the woman. Although they never spoke, they often made eye contact. Although they never smiled, each knew the other's sympathy. Sometimes, when the others weren't looking, the little girl drew fish in the sand with a stick, but she rubbed it out when her classmates came near.

The girl started to grow thinner, too, as she watched the woman each day during her lunch break instead of eating. Her parents fretted and worried, sending a note to her teacher, who followed the girl out during the afternoon one day and discovered why her lunch pail returned to the school room each day as full as it left. The teacher reported to the parents, who marched down to the beach the next day arm in arm; they themselves had enough sense to fear the woman, too, and neither wanted to confront her alone.

The father shouted at the woman as she bent over the pool, hands on her knees, trying to determine if she had seen a shaft of light or the fish. She concentrated too deeply to look up. "Hey!" he shouted, and again, "Hey!" getting louder and angrier as she ignored him. He let go of his wife's arm and rushed towards her, but stopped still as he reached the edge of the pool under the rock. He, too, felt the sacredness of that space, and sputtered helplessly at its edge, calling and shouting about his child as he waved his arms in the air.

She didn't respond, for she was certain she saw the fish under the water, darting back and forth, and this time, she saw the pattern: around in a spiral, flip back on itself, around in a spiral, up... Her lips moved softly as she charted its movement, and she made articulate sound for the first time in seven years.

The father took her speech as a sign that she willfully ignored him. Infuriated, he reached down and scooped up a sharp rock from the edge of the pool, raising it above his head.

...around in a spiral, up...

The rock sailed through the air. He had aimed well, and it flew in an arc that should have hit her head had she not ducked just in time, pushing her arms, torso, and face underwater and wrapping her fingers around the squirming fish as the rock sailed harmlessly over her. She emerged, triumphant, holding the gigantic, silver, wriggling, angry fish, but as she watched it gasp for air, she realised that she didn't want to cook it and eat it; she wanted it to live to give purpose to someone else's life, in another pool, on another continent. Her eyes met the fish's eyes, and they had a moment of understanding, a transfer of wisdom of its own kind, and she bent down to release it.

The father, still infuriated, grabbed another rock and sent it sailing at her, and, guessing at her trajectory, aimed for the surface of the water. The rock skipped off the water and hit the fish, cutting it down the side, exposing bone and gut which spilled into the pool below.

The woman screamed, feeling the pain as though the rock had pierced her own side, and she fell beneath the water. She intended to rise up immediately, but the pool seemed surprisingly deep, and as she fell further and further into its depths, she felt her arms change into fins and her eyes gain the ability to see clearly in the strange, refracted, underwater light.

She hung suspended next to the corpse of the silver fish for a moment, looking at it with understanding, but then the understanding faded and she moved out of the pool, into the sea, and out to another place where someone needed her.

About Llanwyre Laish

Llanwyre Laish's formative years were filled with the fairy tales and myths of Britain and Ireland. As an adult, she spent nine years sandwiched between gargoyles and rare books, racking up degrees while studying the versions of those tales told in the Middle Ages and the nineteenth century. She now teaches academic writing and writes about roleplaying games.

Beachers

Evan Purcell

*Two brothers find an egg on
an isolated beach; they quickly
learn that some things are better
left untouched.*

Simon stood in water three feet deep. He watched the ocean, calm and waiting, stretch out in front of him.

His older brother Ron splashed him from behind. "You know," Ron said, "the human body is 75% water."

Weird thing to say.

"Cool?" Simon said. Right now, he didn't really want to talk. He was having a moment.

"Why don't you come closer to shore?" Ron asked. "I don't want you to..." He didn't bother finishing his sentence. Drown? Sink? It didn't matter. Ron was the older brother, an official teenager now, and Simon had to do whatever he said.

That's what their parents told them, anyway. When the parents weren't around—and let's face it, they were never around—then Ron was in charge.

"Fine," Simon mumbled. He trudged closer to the rocky shore.

An old man wandered toward them. He was the only other person on the beach. And he was horrible. One of his eyes was shriveled and cloudy. He had several jaggedy scars along his face. And his hair—his scraggly, filthy hair—seemed to be poking out of his scalp as if each strand wanted to escape his face.

He was a hermit.

"Careful, boys," he growled.

Ron didn't see him at first, but when the old man started talking, Ron practically jumped out of his skin.

"Careful about what?" Simon asked.

Ron grabbed Simon's arm and pulled him back. He was the big brother, and he needed to stand between Simon and the hermit. He needed to be the shield.

"Creatures," the hermit said. "Hungry ones. You're too young to be out here by yourselves."

"We're not young!" Simon protested. "I'm ten, and Ron is already thirteen."

Ron elbowed him in the stomach. Simon realised, too late, that he'd just told a complete stranger their ages and his brother's first name. He'd broken the number one rule about talking to strangers.

"Go away!" Ron shouted.

The hermit did not go away. In fact, he walked even closer. His old legs moved awkwardly on the rocky ground. He didn't have a cane, but he probably needed one.

"I said go away!" Ron shouted again.

The hermit stopped. He threw both hands in the air, revealing that he was missing several fingers and half-fingers. "I warned you," he said. "I warned you."

And he hobbled away.

"It's okay," Ron said once the old man was good and gone. "I'm here."

"I wasn't scared!" Simon protested.

Ron smiled and tapped him on the shoulder. "Sure, man."

"I wasn't! I never get scared!"

"It's okay," Ron said again. "You're my brother. I promise to always protect you, as long as you do everything I say."

Simon didn't like that last part. "I don't know…"

"Come on!" Ron said and dove into the water.

Simon, as always, followed.

They swam a while, around the rocks. There were things living in the cracks, and if Simon looked hard enough, he could see movement. This close to shore, the water was a little murky and muddy, but still beautiful.

That was when Simon saw the egg.

It was definitely egg-shaped, about eight inches wide and a foot tall. Solid, but flexible. Its surface was covered in spongy nubbins.

Simon jumped up in the water. "Ron," he said. "You gotta see this."

Ron, who seemed disappointed that his brother had made some miraculous discovery instead of him, swam closer.

"Look."

Ron lowered his head under the water. He stayed down for a surprisingly long time. When he surfaced, he said, "Dude. Cool."

"I wanna take it with me."

"No, you can't. There's some living thing in there. Come on, Simon. Use your head."

"But I found it."

"I know. And tonight, we can come back with the underwater camera and take a few pictures, but you are not going to—"

"What do you care about the environment?" Simon asked.

"I care about you," he said. "Just... leave it alone, okay?"

"Fine." As he said it, he felt a hot streak of anger worm through his gut. He hated when his brother called the shots like that. After all, it was just a stupid egg.

They ran along the beach for another hour. But when it was time to go back for lunch, Simon snatched the egg and hid it in his backpack. He made sure Ron wasn't looking, of course.

Ron thought he was so smart, what with his facts about water percentages and stuff, but he had no idea what Simon did.

When they got back to the beach house— parents still not home—Ron fixed them both bologna sandwiches. Simon scarfed his down as if he hadn't eaten in a week. He asked if he could excuse himself, and Ron shrugged. Simon instantly regretted the question, though, because he never asked if he could excuse himself unless their parents were home.

Either way, Ron didn't notice.

Simon went upstairs to his room and locked the door. He needed to play with—no, *examine*—the egg. In the hour since he had taken it out of the ocean, the egg was starting to dry up and smell. Perhaps he should put it in the bathtub.

Naw.

He set it on his dresser, moving his lamp and clock as far away as possible. You know, in case the egg squirted.

It didn't.

It didn't do much of anything.

So Simon poked it with a stick.

Without making a sound—not even a rip or a gloop noise—the egg burst open.

A dozen tiny crabs crawled out, skittered along the floor, skittered up Simon's arms. As he desperately swatted them away, he realised they weren't just crabs. They were... something else.

He couldn't tell how many legs they had, but it had to be at least ten. Probably more. They had little black eyes, glistening and moist, that covered most of the tops of their shells. And their mouths were round, small but lined with teeth.

They bit into his skin.

He writhed around and punched himself. He remembered the old stop, drop, and roll trick from school.

He stopped.

He dropped.

And he rolled around the floor, pounding his

arms desperately on the carpet.

The things made noises, of course, horrible scratching and tearing and chattering noises. He heard a loud crunch and realised that he had squashed one under his shoulder.

Crunch. Another one.

Crunch. Another one.

Once he was sure that every one of them had been smashed—nine in total, not twelve—he checked out the damage left behind. There was a single scratch on his leg, nothing serious, but his arms were another story. The creatures had left behind five bite marks, and they went deep. It looked like a machine had poked holes into his skin, drilling for oil or something. The skin around each wound was torn and puffy.

The first thing he did was bandage up his arms. Normal band-aids were too small, so he had to use the big square ones. Then, he took an aspirin for the pain. Actually, three. He hated that throbbing sensation. And finally, he gathered up the crushed creatures and egg pieces, stuck them in a plastic bag, and buried them behind the house.

A shallow grave.

He even stacked a few rocks on top, just in case those things came back from the dead.

He would've forgotten all about the egg, he would've completely banished it from his mind... except those bite marks made him sick.

At first, he tried to ignore it. Everyone feels dizzy and lightheaded every once in a while. No big deal.

But things quickly got worse.

Simon tried desperately to keep his sickness hidden from Ron and his parents. With his parents, that was pretty easy. They were gone all day doing touristy things. And when they did spend time with their sons, they seldom asked questions.

No, parents were easy. Older brothers, on the other hand...

Ron spent most of his waking hours with Simon. He was supposed to watch after him—Dad said—and he took his responsibilities very seriously.

After a few days, he asked Simon if he was feeling okay.

Simon shrugged and said, "A little queasy. I don't think I've been eating the healthiest food lately." And that was definitely true. But what Simon failed to mention was that he was starting to get shooting pains in his stomach. His mouth was always dry and weird-tasting. And those bite marks continued to throb.

He worried that something had infected him. Those things, those awful little things, must've given him some sort of virus.

Ron didn't know about the bites, though, because Simon was really good at keeping them hidden. He wore long sleeves every day, even though the sun was burning. And whenever Ron asked him a question, Simon would always put on a fake smile and force himself to act happy and normal and *not* sick.

Eventually, he couldn't keep up with the act. He had trouble standing for long periods of time, let alone walking on uneven, rocky ground. He couldn't eat, but he was constantly hungry. He couldn't drink, but he'd never been thirstier in his life.

Simon was falling apart.

One morning, when Simon could barely get out of bed, he told his brother, "Don't get mad, but can you take me to the hospital?"

"I knew something was wrong," Ron said. "What did you do?"

Simon wanted to explain everything, but he didn't have enough strength for full sentences. Instead, he pulled up his shirt and showed Ron his deep, reddish bite marks. They glistened with pus.

"Are those—?"

"The egg," Simon explained, and that was all the explanation necessary.

"Okay, I'm taking you for help right now. Get up."

Ron helped his brother to his feet.

Shaky.

Off-kilter.

Heavy like a sack of meat.

"Don't tell Mom," Simon asked.

"Of course not," Ron said. "This is just you and me. Don't worry. I'll fix you."

Those last three words really helped Simon keep going. Just knowing that his brother would do anything for him... it was all he needed.

When they reached the main road, Ron turned right, not left. If they went left, they'd go to the main street, where there would be doctors and hospitals and all sorts of medical help.

But they didn't go in that direction. They went the other way. They went toward the beach where everything started.

"Ron?"

"Trust me, okay."

And he did. Simon trusted his brother with his life. He just wished they had turned the other way.

The two brothers were at the beach now. Simon leaned against his older brother's side, struggling to keep pace. His breathing was raggedy and loud. Painful, too. They walked close enough to the ocean to get their sneakers wet.

"Why are we...?" Simon asked.

"Trust me," Ron said. "We're getting help."

He led his little brother further and further away from their beach house. Further and further away from anything, really. By now, they'd reached the lonely stretch of beach where Simon had first discovered the egg.

Simon was starting to get nervous. His thoughts were frazzled from the infection—his vision was fuzzy, too—but the fear cut through that like a beam of light.

Why is he taking me here?

Does he want to return me to the sea?

The idea was ludicrous, of course. His brother cared for him, looked out for him like a worried parent. When their real parents were nowhere to be seen, Ron was always watching, for better or for worse. Still, Simon got the distinct feeling that his brother was planning to leave him here, to push him into the ocean where the creatures would finish what they started... where their little bites would turn into big bites... and then...

Simon didn't notice the old man until he was a few feet away. The hermit! That was why Ron had taken them there. He knew that the old man would have answers.

Still, a hospital would've been better...

"Why, it's my old friends," the hermit said. "My old friends came back to me."

"Sir," Ron said. And Simon couldn't hear the rest. He was too woozy to concentrate. All he could hear were the pounding waves, both on the beach and in his head.

Whatever Ron said, though, it worked, because the hermit waved them forward. "Follow me."

He took the two boys to a shack just on the other side of a rocky ledge. It was made from rusted sheet metal and warped wood. Within a few years, it would wash away. But for now, it was his home.

"In!" the hermit said. "In! In!"

Ron and Simon entered. There wasn't a door, just a dirty curtain hanging over a doorway. Ron pushed it aside. Simon leaned against the wall, even though it could barely support its own weight, let alone the weight of a ten-year-old.

"The little one is sick," the hermit said. "He needs help."

"Yeah," Ron whispered. He showed the old man the wounds on Simon's arms.

"What did this?" the hermit asked.

Ron looked at his brother. He wouldn't be able to answer this question. Only Simon could answer it.

"Creatures. Little crabs. Skittering. So many legs."

"Did they have black eyes?" the hermit asked. "Hundreds of 'em?"

"Yes."

Ron chimed in. "We found this egg on the beach. Just a little bit away from here. I told him not to touch it, but..."

The hermit shook his head. "You did a bad thing," he said. "You did the baddest thing you could possibly do."

"Why?" Simon asked. He knew they shouldn't have gone to this horrible place. They should've gone to the hospital, where real medical professionals could give him a few pills and send him on his way.

No. This felt wrong. Very wrong.

The hermit clicked his tongue. He didn't look at Simon or Roy. If this were a real doctor in a real hospital, he would've looked at his patient before delivering the bad news.

Simon gulped.

"Those creatures you saw," the hermit explained, "they're bad news. Around here, we call 'em 'beachers'."

"Beachers?" Ron joined in. "That's a stupid name."

"There's nothing stupid about them," the hermit said. "They don't think, at least not the way you and I do. They're ancient creatures, and they act on instinct. Feed, kill, grow. And boy, do they grow. One day, they're small as dust mites, and the next..." He clapped his hands really loudly. "You should not have disturbed them."

"But..."

"I used to have a family, too, you know," the hermit said. "And then the beachers, well..." His voice trailed off. At that moment, he looked directly at Simon. One of his eyes—the glossy gray one—blinked, while the other stayed open.

"But it's okay," Roy said, trying to hide the panic in his voice. "Simon crushed them all. Right, Simon? You crushed 'em, right?"

"Yeah," Simon said. "Like a dozen of them. I got every single one."

"And they didn't hurt you?" the hermit asked. "They didn't get anywhere near your mouth or your ear holes, right?"

What a funny question! Simon had to think back, all the way back to six days ago, when those horrible things crawled all over his body. He remembered them crawling up his arms, tearing at his skin. He remembered them swarming his feet. But he didn't remember—thank God—any of them getting near his face.

Simon was queasy already, but that simple memory seemed to sap whatever strength he had left. He crumpled to the ground, and he would've landed hard if Ron didn't catch him.

Ron always caught him when he fell.

"No, sir," Simon mumbled. "They didn't... crawl into my mouth or ears." Saying that sentence out loud made him feel ever worse.

The hermit squinted... or winked, it was hard to tell. He studied Simon's pale body. Then he slowly began to back away. "Son," he said, "your arms…"

Simon looked at the dime-sized wounds. He should've put bandages on them today, but he'd forgotten. They'd gotten much worse in the last few hours. The surrounding skin was green now, not red. If he looked close enough, he could see the wounds throbbing.

"They bit me," Simon said. "I…"

"You don't think the bite marks are infected, do you?" Ron asked. He held his brother tight.

The hermit shook his head sadly. "Those aren't bite marks, I'm afraid."

Simon could barely swallow his own spit. The world seemed so much fuzzier now. He started to ask a question, but the words wouldn't come out.

Ron had to speak for him. "Then what are they?" he asked.

"Entrance wounds," the hermit said.

At first, Simon didn't quite understand. His brain was too fuzzy. Then the words sank in.

"Like I said," the hermit continued, "the beachers grow extremely fast. And before they hatch, they need to be in an environment with a lot of water. That's their… well, habitat. Judging by the size of your wounds, it looks like they had about a week left before they were big enough to hatch."

"When you say hatch…" Ron said.

"I mean that these creatures will hatch out of your brother. They are incubating inside him, in his watery innards, and when they are ready… Well, hatch is probably the best word."

Simon was so woozy now, he could barely

make out the hermit's voice. But he heard enough to understand the basics. Maybe it would've been better if he didn't hear anything at all.

"Yes, sir," the hermit continued. He was talking directly to Ron now, as if Simon was completely beyond hope. "They have about a week until they're ready. Now tell me, how long ago did they enter your brother's body?"

Simon had enough strength for two more words: "Six days."

About Evan Purcell

Evan Purcell is an American living and working in rural China, a land of ancient traditions, friendly people, and absolutely no cheese in a hundred-mile radius. Except for that last part, he really enjoys his life abroad. He also writes a lot of horror and sci-fi short stories, as well as the occasional romance novel. You can read about his travels and his weirdly eclectic writing at EvanPurcell.blogspot.com. And if you see him walking down the street, please offer him some American cheese. He misses it so much.

Made in the USA
Charleston, SC
18 August 2014